— I can't watch!

LEMUR DREAMER

Courtney Dicmas

templar publishing

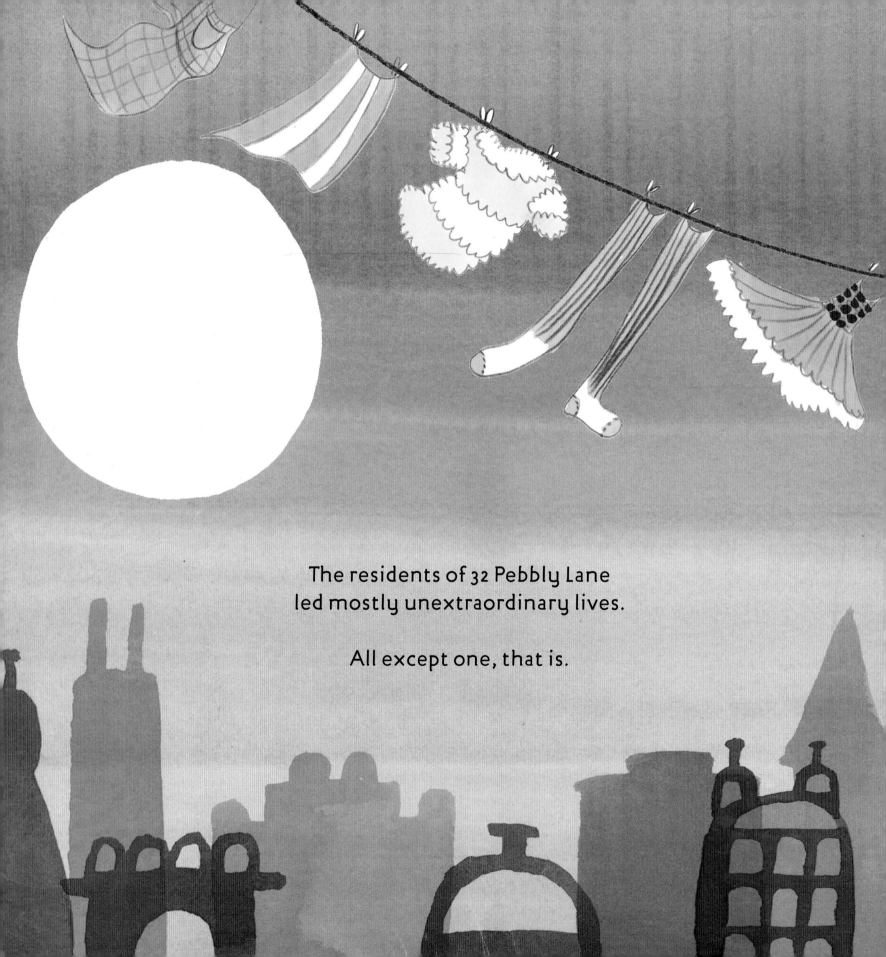

The residents of 32 Pebbly Lane
led mostly unextraordinary lives.

All except one, that is.

Louis, who lived on
the very top floor,

had the unfortunate habit...

of **sleepwalking!**

Every night, fast asleep, Louis wandered out his front door, snoozed around the other apartments, and snuffled back to bed.

It wasn't a problem at first.

The neighbours were very understanding.

But as time went on,

Louis went on wandering,
until one night he snoozed
down a washing line...

and snuffled
right out onto
Pebbly Lane!

sssh

This was getting out of hand.
"Where's Louis going?" whispered his friends.
"What shall we do?"

"There's just one thing for it," said Little Bird.
"We will have to walk with him."

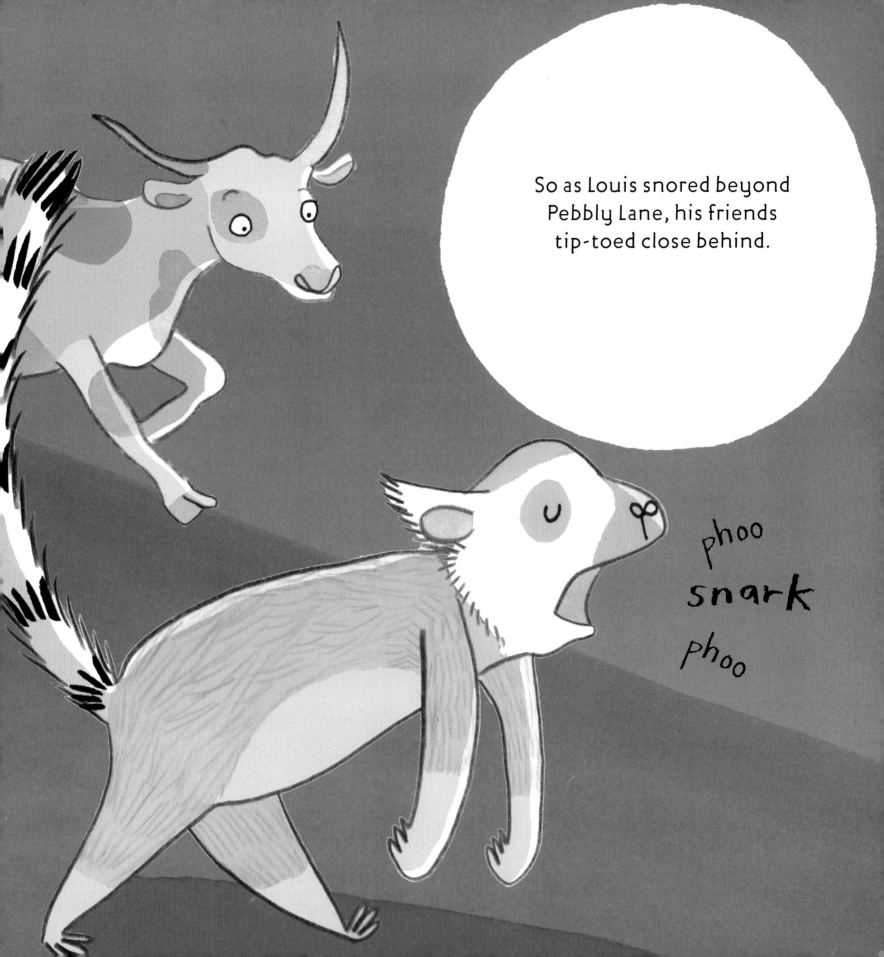

So as Louis snored beyond Pebbly Lane, his friends tip-toed close behind.

No one knew what he was dreaming of.

But whatever it was...

and wherever he went...

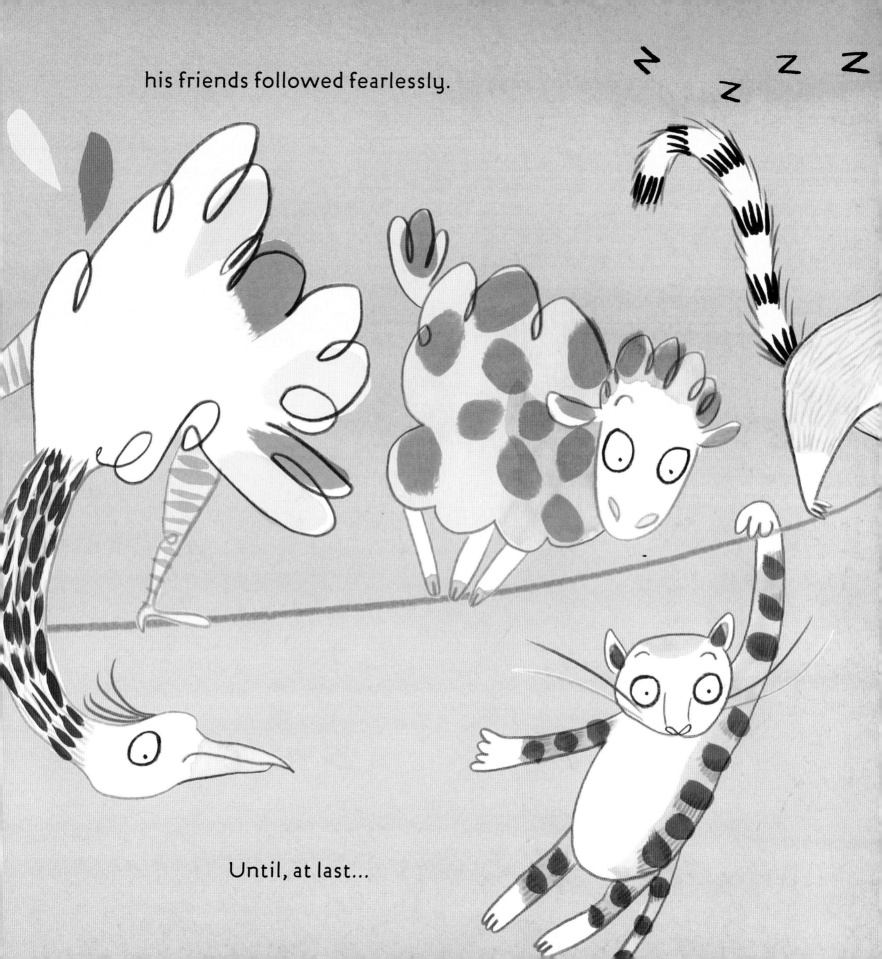

his friends followed fearlessly.

Until, at last...

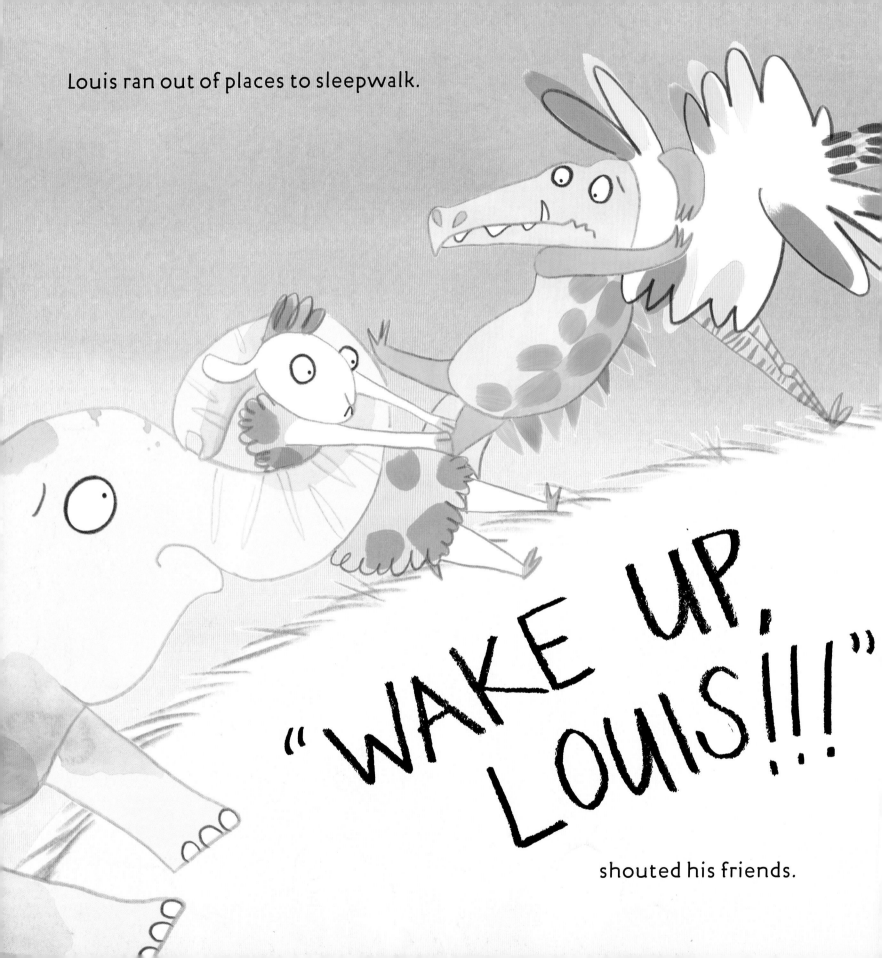

Louis ran out of places to sleepwalk.

"WAKE UP, LOUIS!!!"

shouted his friends.

But Louis was still fast asleep.
Could they reach him in time?

OOOF!

Safely back on the cliff,
lucky Louis sat up,
blinked twice
and YAWNED.

"I had the MOST amazing dreams
last night," he said.

"I dreamed I climbed the steepest slopes of Mount Everest..."

"... and dazzled everyone on the tightrope at the circus."

"Then, I was just about
to go scuba diving
on the Great Barrier Reef,
when something
stopped me."

"But where am I?
And what are you
all doing here?

Hang on a minute..."

"I've been sleepwalking again!"

Louis felt terrible. He'd caused his friends so much trouble.
But they didn't mind. They loved Louis, even with all his snoozing and snuffling.

So to cheer him up, the next day his friends decided to get Louis a special present.

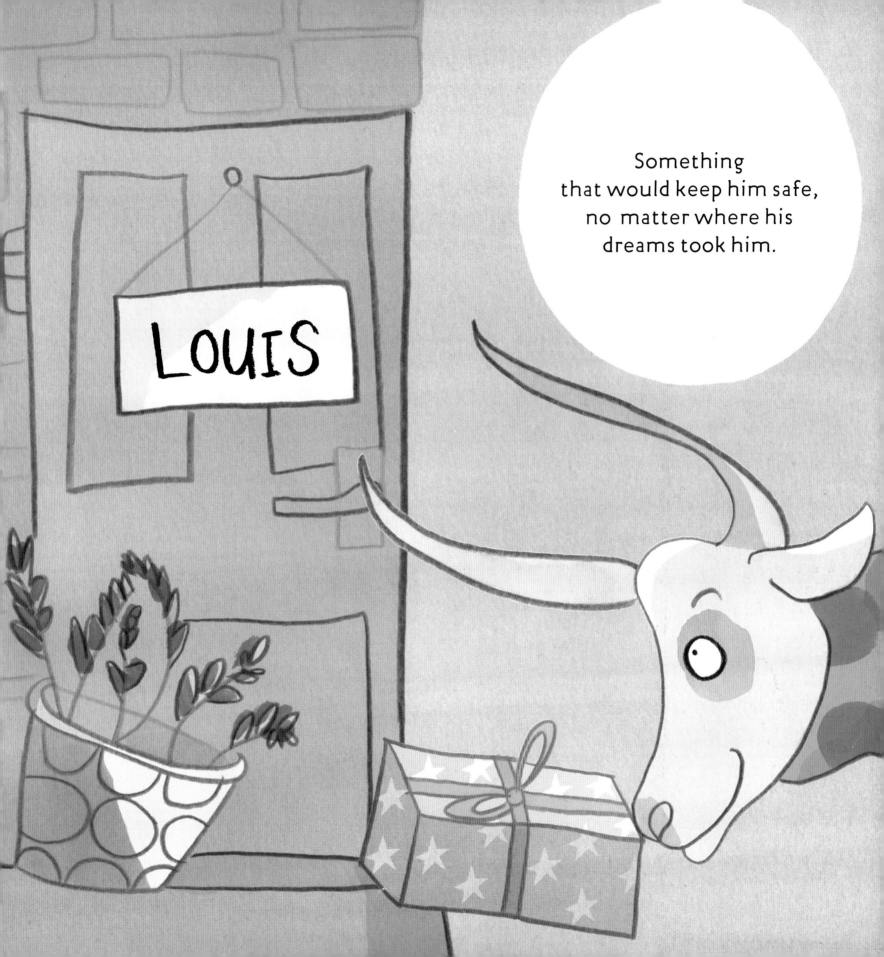

Something
that would keep him safe,
no matter where his
dreams took him.